Dear Parents and Educators,  W9-BAA-651

Welcome to Penguin Young Readers! As parents and educators, you know that each child develops at his or her own pace—in terms of speech, critical thinking, and, of course, reading. Penguin Young Readers recognizes this fact. As a result, each Penguin Young Readers book is assigned a traditional easy-to-read level (1–4) as well as a Guided Reading Level (A–P). Both of these systems will help you choose the right book for your child. Please refer to the back of each book for specific leveling information. Penguin Young Readers features esteemed authors and illustrators, stories about favorite characters, fascinating nonfiction, and more!

Angelina Ballerina™
Angelina Has the Hiccups!

LEVEL 2

GUIDED READING LEVEL **I**

This book is perfect for a **Progressing Reader** who:
- can figure out unknown words by using picture and context clues;
- can recognize beginning, middle, and ending sounds;
- can make and confirm predictions about what will happen in the text; and
- can distinguish between fiction and nonfiction.

Here are some **activities** you can do during and after reading this book:
- Problem/Solution: In this story, Angelina gets a case of the hiccups before her ballet show. This is the problem. Discuss the solution to Angelina's problem.
- Make Connections: Alice is nervous before the show. Have you ever been nervous? Why? Write a paragraph with the child about the experience and how the child overcame his or her nervousness.

Remember, sharing the love of reading with a child is the best gift you can give!

—Bonnie Bader, EdM
Penguin Young Readers program

*Penguin Young Readers are leveled by independent reviewers applying the standards developed by Irene Fountas and Gay Su Pinnell in *Matching Books to Readers: Using Leveled Books in Guided Reading*, Heinemann, 1999.

HiT entertainment

Penguin Young Readers
Published by the Penguin Group
Penguin Group (USA) Inc., 375 Hudson Street, New York, New York 10014, USA
Penguin Group (Canada), 90 Eglinton Avenue East, Suite 700, Toronto, Ontario M4P 2Y3, Canada
(a division of Pearson Penguin Canada Inc.)
Penguin Books Ltd, 80 Strand, London WC2R 0RL, England
Penguin Ireland, 25 St Stephen's Green, Dublin 2, Ireland (a division of Penguin Books Ltd)
Penguin Group (Australia), 707 Collins Street, Melbourne, Victoria 3008, Australia
(a division of Pearson Australia Group Pty Ltd)
Penguin Books India Pvt Ltd, 11 Community Centre, Panchsheel Park, New Delhi—110 017, India
Penguin Group (NZ), 67 Apollo Drive, Rosedale, Auckland 0632, New Zealand
(a division of Pearson New Zealand Ltd)
Penguin Books (South Africa), Rosebank Office Park, 181 Jan Smuts Avenue,
Parktown North 2193, South Africa
Penguin China, B7 Jiaming Center, 27 East Third Ring Road North,
Chaoyang District, Beijing 100020, China

Penguin Books Ltd, Registered Offices: 80 Strand, London WC2R 0RL, England

Library of Congress Control Number: 2006002436

ISBN 978-0-448-44389-8   10 9 8 7 6 5 4 3 2 1

Angelina Has the Hiccups!

by Katharine Holabird
based on the illustrations by Helen Craig

Penguin Young Readers
An Imprint of Penguin Group (USA) Inc.

Angelina loves to dance.

Angelina dances

on the way to school . . .

in the playground . . .

even at bedtime!

Angelina has a very best friend.

Her name is Alice.

Alice loves to dance, too.

Angelina and Alice go

to ballet school every week.

Their teacher is Miss Lilly.

Angelina and Alice

love Miss Lilly.

Today Miss Lilly has a surprise.

"We will give a performance,"

she tells the class.

"The dance is called

The Flower Princesses

and the Dragon."

"Yippee!" everyone shouts.

All the ballet students are
in the show.

Cousin Henry is the dragon.

"ROAR!" Henry roars proudly.

"I am a very scary dragon."

Angelina and the other
mouselings are flower princesses.

Angelina is Rose.

She has a wand with a rose.

Alice is Violet.

Her wand has a violet on top.

Miss Lilly shows her students

the steps in the dance.

The flower princesses twirl and

leap across the room.

Henry the dragon
takes big dragon steps.
Thud! Thud! Thud!
"Practice makes perfect,"
Miss Lilly says.

17

Every morning, Angelina

gets up early.

"Watch me twirl and leap,"

she says.

"Not in the kitchen!"

Mrs. Mouseling reminds her.

Every day after school,

Angelina and Alice practice.

They know all

the steps by heart.

Today the mouselings try

on their costumes.

"What if I forget the steps?"

says Alice.

Angelina says, "Do not worry.

Just follow me."

Now Alice feels much better.

Henry has his costume, too.

But he will not let anyone see it.

"I want it to be a surprise,"

he says.

On the day of the show,

Angelina is very excited.

Soon Alice arrives.

"Hi," says Alice.

"Hi!" says Angelina.

Then out comes a big—HICCUP!

Hiccup! Hiccup! Hiccup!

Oh no!

Angelina has the hiccups.

"Hold your breath," says Alice.

Angelina holds her breath.

"HICCUP!" she hiccups.

"Try a spoonful of sugar,"

says Mrs. Mouseling.

Angelina eats a spoonful

of sugar.

"HICCUP!" Angelina hiccups.

Then Angelina hiccups all the

way to the theater.

"Blow in a paper bag,"

says Miss Lilly.

Angelina blows in a paper bag.

"HICCUP!" she hiccups.

Angelina puts on her costume.

HICCUP!

Angelina puts on her
ballet slippers.

HICCUP!

Angelina gets her rose wand.

HICCUP!

The music is starting.

"HICCUP!" Angelina hiccups.

Angelina is ready to cry.

How can she be a

hiccuping ballerina?

"ROAR!"

A scary dragon jumps out

at Angelina.

Angelina jumps, too.

But it is only Henry—

Henry the dragon!

"I told Henry to try scaring away

your hiccups," says Alice.

"Did it work?"

Angelina smiles.

No more hiccups!

Onstage, Angelina and Alice

twirl and leap.

The flower princesses turn

the scary dragon into

a friendly dragon.

After the dance,

Angelina hugs Henry.

"Thank you," she says.

"ROAR!" Henry roars proudly.